WHEN THE ANGEL
DESERVES TO DIE

When The Angel Deserves To Die

Florent FSan PORTE

First Printing: July 2014
ISBN 978-1-312-36545-2

Florent FSan PORTE, Alice Productions
Burnaby, BC, Canada
www.fsanporte.com

I'd like to give special thanks to a few people without whom such a project would have never been possible.

Amber, for her support and for putting up with me.
Shalini, for her presence and life advices.
John Capone, for being one of the reasons I am the kind of artist I am today.

All the people who have supported me and my work, and still support me today.

CONTENTS

PREFACE

Back in November 2011, I was working on calendar featuring illustrations especially made for the occasion. One of the images was titled "The Guardians Of Wonderland", and would soon after become one of the reasons for this book.

I always had a particular liking for Lewis Carroll's "Alice's Adventures In Wonderland", so much so that some would probably comment that my liking is actually closer to a mild obsession, which I could hardly argue. And so, as I was working on the particular illustration mentioned above, an idea formed in my mind; idea which soon developed into a vague story including my own versions of the famous Alice followed by her queer companions. A few months later, I decided to turn this simple image and concepts within it into a full sized story, and ultimately a novel. Since then, the project has grown even bigger and it still occupies most of my personal time. At the time I am writing these lines, the novel is not quite finished yet, but it is well under way and should see the printing press in the near future.

What does this have anything to do with the current book? Not much, yet quite a lot at the same time.

When I decided to write "The Guardians Of Wonderland", I wanted to use a concept close to the original publication by Lewis Carroll – at least in its form. The text will be subject to wacky formatting and illustrations to accompany the story. But earlier in the year 2014, I had to consider several facts in view of the size this project has become, the main one being that I had no real idea how to handle it on a more technical level –especially regarding formatting and including the illustrations.

So I decided that it would be good to go through the exercise at least once before finishing "The Guardians", albeit on a smaller scale. As I was pondering this possibility, I was reading some old material of mine and going over old notes. Out of all those pages, three of my older short stories stood out and that is when I decided to bring them together into the book you are holding right now, along with specially made illustrations.

I do not claim to be a writer. In fact, when I present myself as an artist, I usually bring my digital work on the front and only sometimes mention my writing. But writing is –and has always been, an important part of my creation process and ultimately of my evolution as an artist. To add to this, I had to rewrite and adapt the short stories in this book from their original versions, which I had written in French (my first language) and update them to fit the format I wanted to try here.

The short stories you are about to read are all works of fiction, but have elements inspired by either real life experiences or real people (or even both) turned into something more "fantastic" for the sake of telling a story. This makes these stories quite special and personal, but will hopefully reach all kinds of readers in their own way.

Finally, what better way to end this book almost the way it started? I decided to include an excerpt from the unfinished first chapter of "The Guardians Of Wonderland" because I have been talking about for so long that I thought it was only fair to give out a little piece of it.

I hope that you will enjoy these stories as much as I enjoyed writing and illustrating them.

"The Guardians Of Wonderland" - November 2011

Amuse A Muse

AMUSE
A
MUSE

She was running. She was running naked in the street dimly lit by a few weak lights. She could hear the footsteps following her as they were closing in with every passing second. She was running for her life.

She lost her balance and her attacker took hold of her, pushing her against the cold wall, turning her around so she would be facing him. She couldn't see his face as her attention was focused on the knife he was waving in front of her eyes. The first tears appeared and were soon flowing down her scared face.

"Enough!" A voice said from behind the aggressor.

A man was standing there a few feet away, wearing a dark linen coat and a black hat. He had a backpack hanging on one of his shoulders. He slowly put it down on the ground before coming closer to the strange couple.

"Leave this young woman alone." The newcomer said. "Or you might regret it."

The man holding the knife grumbled an insult as he leapt on him. They fought for a few seconds only, until the newcomer grabbed the knife and stabbed the pervert's cheek with a blank face. He pulled violently, cutting through the cheek with ease as blood gushed everywhere. The man screamed, bringing his hands to his face, covering his now split cheek as blood was filling his mouth. But the newcomer didn't stop there, now stabbing his victim in the abdomen several times. He moved the blade around a bit as it was slicing through the bloody guts, moving the weapon upward as a butcher would do on a piece of meat. The man fell to his knees, blood flowing from his open stomach to the rhythm of his still beating heart, until he collapsed on the ground groaning as life was leaking out of his body.

The newcomer had already lost all interest in the dying man and he turned around to face the frightened woman who had not moved from the wall. He dropped the knife and slowly came closer, showing the palms of his hands as though he wanted to express that he meant no harm.

"My name is Frank…" He said in a voice almost too sweet to be real. "You have nothing to fear now."

He took his coat off and wrapped her in it. She didn't object to it, glad that she could finally cover her exposed body.

She didn't see his hand go in the pocket as he was taking her in his arms. She didn't see the syringe coming towards her face rapidly, the needle plunging in her neck. A few seconds later she had lost all sensations in her body as Frank was laying her down carefully on the ground.

He stayed next to her, a knee on the ground as he observed her naked body. Not like the pervert a few minutes earlier, but with the trained eye of a surgeon looking for the imperfection to correct. The young woman could not move but she was fully conscious, fear in her eyes. She was horrified. She could not feel those hands feeling various parts of her body, sometimes intimate.

"Hmm…" He whispered. "If you're lucky, you'll do just fine. No need to be afraid, really."

He got up, and slowly walked to his backpack on the ground. He opened it and took out a plastic bag before going back to kneel next to the woman. From the plastic bag came out a measuring tape and he soon started to take her measurements. Nothing was forgotten, from the length of her legs, even her toes, the size of her breasts, of her waist and hips, of her arms and fingers. As he was doing so, he was writing his observations on a notepad made of yellow paper. He grabbed a strand of her hair between two fingers, as if he were gauging the thickness of each hair. Then he observed her in silence for a long minute.

Her pale skin was almost glowing in the darkness of the street, the bright red hair giving even more depth to her scared emerald eyes.

He took out yet another notepad from the bag and read the numbers written on it, comparing them with the ones he had just noted. After a few seconds, disappointment was seen on his face and he started to check again on some parts of the woman's defenseless body, only to find the same numbers. He shrugged, putting the notepads back in his bag before pulling out a wide knife similar to those a butcher would use. He looked at the woman with round and glistening eyes, smiling at her.

"Your waist is a tad too large and your legs a tad not enough… Ah well, that's too bad…"

And without any warning, he chopped her head off with three strong blows, blood gushing on him and on the ground.

Once he was done, he got up slowly, looking down at the mutilated corpse. From the bag he took out a smaller knife and started to open the woman's abdomen before plunging his hands inside, pulling out her innards. He sliced here and there before putting the pieces in a Ziploc bag.

He got up again and took his clothes off slowly as if time did not matter until he was himself completely naked in the street. He made a bunch with his soiled clothes, wiped his hands and his face with a towel he had taken out of his bag, and threw it on top of the clothes on the ground. From the bag he took out a clear bottle. He opened it and emptied the content on the clothes before lighting a match and throwing it on there as well. The fire was instant, the bright light from it flowing on his naked body, giving his cold eyes a strange glow as a faint smile came on his lips.

Before the fire died out, he dressed with a new set of clothes. All his "tools" were put in a garbage bag and he walked away without a look for any of his victims. Soon he was in his car, driving away.

The house in the suburbs was covered by the darkness of the night. The garage door slid open and Frank parked his car inside. He made sure the door was fully closed before stepping inside the house, welcomed by an ugly black dog, apparently too well fed. From the garbage bag, the man took out the Ziploc bag containing the bloody guts that he dropped in the dog's bowl.

"Don't eat too fast, you'll get sick."

He then walked to his basement, turning the light on. The room was practically empty except for a few shelves covered in rusty tools. And except for the table in the middle, and the naked body on top of it.

He came closer and observed the corpse which was apparently quite fresh. He ran the tip of his fingers on the still pink cheeks with a smile. He brushed the red hair for several minutes before fixing the already perfect makeup.

"I'm sorry my dear, I know time is of the essence, but the body wasn't good enough. We'll have to wait a little bit more. I hope you can forgive me…"

He was standing there next to the dead woman's face, moving his fingers on the soft skin in spite of the rigidity that had started to do its work. A smile on his face, he could feel the warmth enveloping him; he could feel the arms wrapping themselves around him, hugging him from behind; he could feel the sharp blades running on his chest, a few drops of blood flowing down his abdomen.

And he could hear her. He could hear her words. Those loving words whispered to his ear, those words telling him what to do, reassuring him.

He held his hands up to the ceiling, overwhelmed by his feelings and this affection she was giving him. She was his. He would do anything she would ask of him. She was his mind, his will.

Madness came upon him. And she was his Muse.

The Theory of the Razorblade

THE
THEORY
OF
THE

RAZORBLADE

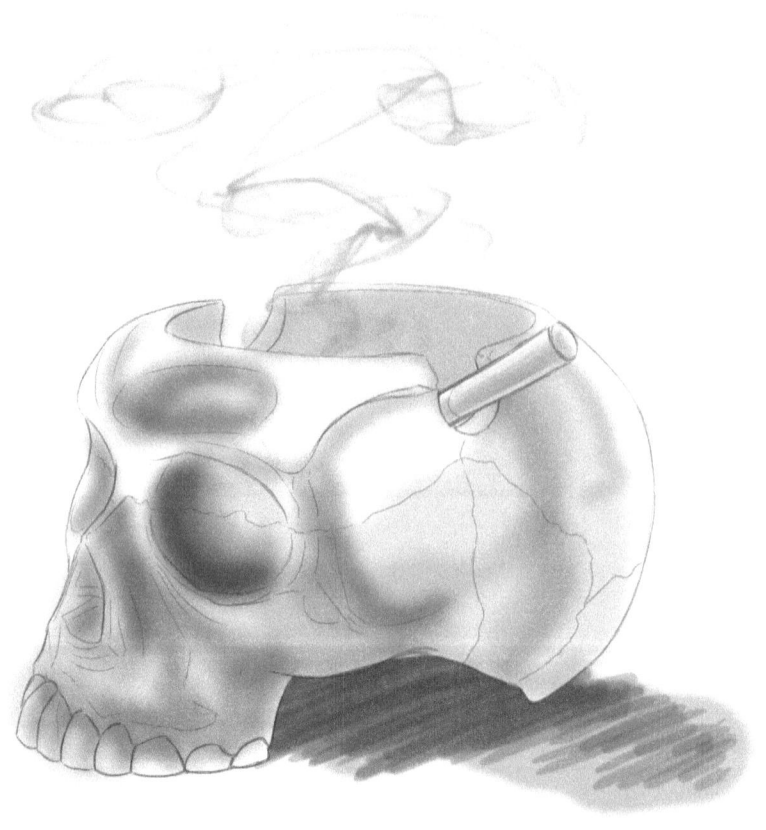

Researches on suicide are many, and more are regularly released by very academic entities. Pages of numbers and statistics are compiled among even more percentages and mass studies. But what about the individuals? Did we ask this boy, girl, man or woman who was not too clumsy and actually succeeded? Did we ask them why they ended up doing it? No, of course not, and for obvious reasons. We could throw an infinite amount of hypotheses as to why someone would commit suicide without necessarily finding the answer, or knowing we found it since we can't ask the dead anymore.

To tell you the truth, this point of view is not what matters in my opinion. As soon as we start talking about "people" as a group, a phenomenon has no real value anymore, it has no direct emotional impact, it doesn't shock. But if we start looking at a particular individual, a person... All of a sudden, it is a lot more colourful, a lot more vibrant. What if this person was someone you knew? A family member, a dear friend, or someone you loved more than your own death?...

It was when he started crying that she suddenly woke up, dropping the blade to the floor where it bounced a few times. He had called her by her name for long minutes. As a response, he could only hear her breathing, and the silence. A heavy silence that had nothing to do with what it usually was, this silence that often made them feel like the distance between them was not as large, a silence that made them forget they were only on the phone.

The more he had called her name, the heavier the silence had become, and the angrier he was getting. Anger not towards her, but against the distance and the fact that he could not do anything about it. He could not bear not being able to find the words that would stop her. He knew what she was doing, he could see her in his mind, the blade in her hand. Powerless, held by the fear of losing her, he started crying, dropping to the ground, sitting there and staring at the dirty pavement.

It was when he started crying that she suddenly woke up, dropping the blade to the floor where it bounced a few times. As though his sobs had pulled her back into this world from the dark waters of her own insanity. She remembered her promise to never hurt him, and she started to cry as well. But he now was the one who was lost in darkness, disconnected. He opened his eyes and wrapped himself in his long coat before getting up, helping himself with the wall as though he was too weak to just stand up. Slowly, he was coming back from this endless abyss his soul was. He wanted to hold her, but he could not. He wiped his tears with the sleeve of his coat and mumbled a few reassuring words. But the damage was done and would never be fixed.

There must be as many reasons to commit suicide as there are individuals who attempt it, or even succeed. I won't even try to list them here, I won't even give examples. It would be useless to do so and point of views would be too diverse on the matter. And again, people are not interesting to me. I would rather focus on individuals, on persons. Everybody knows someone who attempted –or succeeded to take their own lives, and each person has their own sensibility, if any at all.

But I feel like digressing a bit, or maybe widening the scope. To jump from the tenth floor of a building, to hang oneself with the phone cable, to let oneself drown and sink in a lake, to jump in front of a speeding train, to swallow a good amount of dangerous pills, to simply shoot a bullet in one's own mouth or head... So many ways to do it. My personal favourite is the razorblade. It feels more civilized. Does it hurt? Not necessarily...

It was very late at night, as always when he was coming home. He had thought about her during the day and even more so in the evening as the sun was disappearing behind the horizon. A strange and oppressing feeling had taken him aback, as if he knew something had happened to her.

Their relationship was not what it had been years before, and some of it was because of him. He had no excuse, and he was not trying to find any. He was tired of fighting, and so he had said nothing when she had been waiting for his words. He regretted it but there was nothing to be done about it now. Darkness, deeper today than usual, was eating him every day a bit more.

He was surprised to find someone in front of his door when the lights in the halls of the old building came on. A figure laying on the ground. He recognized her right away in spite of her messy hair and her torn and dirty clothes. She looked up, empty eyes staring at him as he arrived next to her. He was worried, but neither of them said a word. He helped her stand up, only to see that she was covered in blood. He quickly dragged her inside and tried to get a few words from her, something that would explain why she was like this in the middle of the night. But she did not say anything, gazing at the void in front of her as though she was not part of this world.

He took off his heavy coat and his jacket before pulling the sleeves of his shirt up. She did not blink when he started to look for the origin of all the blood that was covering her and her clothes. He knew nothing had happened to her: she had done it to herself. He pulled on her woolen sweater and took it off of her before looking at her left arm. He knew of her habit, quite an unfortunate one indeed.

He was not surprised to find a dozen of cuts all along her limbs, some deeper than others, from her wrists to her shoulders. He did not ask for a reason, she already had explained it to him once.

He stared at her tired eyes before rearranging her hair so he could see her face better. He kneeled in front of her and started to take the rest of her clothes off slowly, not wanting to frighten her. He was talking to her in a gentle voice, explaining to her why he was doing this to her.

"We need to clean up the blood and your wounds. We'll get you in the shower then we'll put you in bed and you're going to sleep because you are tired. You need to sleep, we can talk about it tomorrow if you feel like it..."

Once she was naked, he dragged her to the bathroom, to the shower cubicle. He turned on the water, making sure it was neither too warm nor too cold. She did not move when he started to clean her up, not caring about his own clothes becoming heavy from the water as he was standing under the shower with her. He carefully washed her lacerated arm as she was watching him absently, still silent. Once he deemed her to be clean enough, he stopped the water and stared at her eyes again. She looked back at him, clear eyes locked to his, as dark as his soul. She frowned lightly as life seemed to come back in her eyes, and tears formed. He brought his hand to her pale cheek, trying to calm her down as she was slowly coming back to reality. She moved closer until she was against him, her face buried in his soaked shirt. He wrapped his arms around her, embracing her tight.

"Why doesn't it hurt?..." She whispered. "Why is it not working this time?... Am I dead?..."

He could not find the right words to tell her, so he waited for her to calm down. He waited for a few more seconds and slowly let go of her before grabbing a towel and carefully drying her. He brought her a large t-shirt and pulled it over her head as she weakly slid her arms in the sleeves. He took her hand and lead her to the bedroom and to the large bed. She had stopped talking, as if there really was nothing to say. He laid her down on the bed, then proceeded to disinfect the wounds on her arm, covering the deeper ones with band aids. He looked down at her as he got up, turning around and walking toward the bathroom again. She stopped him with her frail voice.

"You're coming back, right?... You're not leaving me?..."

"Yes I'm coming back." He said with a faint smile. "I just need to change."

Back in the bathroom, he took off his clothes until his eyes fell on his razor. It was an old kind of razor his father had given him, himself getting it from his father. He took out the blade from it and stared at it for long seconds.

"The theory of the razorblade, huh?..." he whispered before throwing it in the bin next to the sink.

He put on new clothes and walked back to the bedroom where the young girl had not moved. She looked at him as he climbed in the bed next to her and switched the lights off. He kissed her forehead and whispered something to her. He lay down and closed his eyes.

She turned to him and brought her wounded arm on his chest.

He opened his eyes again and gazed at her through the darkness before turning to her as well, wrapping his arms around her. She fell asleep first, and he did soon after. But the night never did end.

The razorblade is a very private thing sometimes. As much a kind of intellectual masturbation than a physical one. Is it a pleasure to hurt oneself? Some will say yes, others will say no. But when you hurt, it is a physical pain no one else than yourself can feel, it is a pain you keep for yourself, you cannot share it no matter how much someone else want to take it from you. If I cut my veins, it may hurt, but the pain would be mine. The blade would cut through my skin, my flesh, not yours. And if you did the same thing at the same time, you might feel something totally different. You might enjoy it while I hate it.

One can use the razorblade to hurt, to wake up, to feel real. To think that this blood flowing, this life leaking away, is nobody else's. To search for one's life, to hurt and never regret.

In the end, the razorblade is a very selfish thing...

When The Angel
Deserves To Die

WHEN THE ANGEL DESERVES TO DIE

His name had been written after all the others for an hour already. But he would escape it. He was the Master and the curse would not claim him the same way it had taken away hundreds of ignorant souls during the past years, during the past centuries.

Everywhere he went, he brought it with him, shoved deep in his battered jacket that was so old it didn't even have any real color anymore. A hole by the left elbow, the leather stained with wine or other alcohol. He had not slept for the past two weeks at least. He had not eaten, barely showered. But was he really conscious of it? Probably not any more than he had become a mad man, believing he now was the Master of the world. He had the whole population at his feet and he could decide of their fate. He did not have the scythe Death had, but he possessed a much worse, more efficient weapon. The Book.

What he did not know though, blinded by his madness and his lack of sleep giving him bloodshot eyes, was that he was not all powerful. The Book possessed him, consumed him, it was burning the last piece of sanity that had not left his soul yet.

The Book would kill him the same way it had killed its owners before. Those pages would call on the Dark Angel to change this mad man into meat for the worms.

His name had been written after all the others for an hour already.

I was there when this man wandered towards the railway, his back bent, his hands deep in his pocket as though he wanted to protect them from the cold. He was not even conscious of where he was going as he was following the railway aside the empty warehouse. This line had not been used for the past ten years, and it was invaded by weeds growing between the rocks, some of them so strong that they bent the wooden planks. There always was someone walking his dog in this area during the afternoon. But not today. No elder walking around, a cap on his head, a rolled cigarette between the dry lips. Not even a single rodent looking for food in the green leaves. It was as though they had known.

I saw the creature and *his* majestic black wings move from a large rock as the glowing feathers seemed to have a life of their own. But the man didn't see. As soon as he put his foot on the stones between the railways, he lost his balance and twisted his ankle, groaning as he fell on the rails. He screamed both from anger and from pain as he had probably broken a couple of ribs in his fall. He wiggled on the ground like a fish out of the water until he finally stopped, lying flat on his back, gazing at the sky with his drunken eyes.

He finally saw *him*. The black-winged Angel was standing above him as if *he* had literally appeared there, showing *himself* in all *his* majesty. *His* black linen robe was tight around *his* thin waist, covering *his* long and pale legs. *His* skin seemed to reflect the light, or maybe it was producing its own light, cold and hard. *His* face had elegant, almost feminine lines. *His* toned arms were on *his* sides, *his* wrists circled with ornate bracelets, sparkling as if they were also made of light. *His* mouth, barely visible in the brightness of *his* face showed no emotion. But *his* eyes… Two black jewels with no reflections, much like two holes in the white face. Two terrifying pearls, cold and empty for someone who seemed definitely alive. *His* thin eyebrows joined together in a frown and an expression of hatred formed in the two orbs. *His* long dark hair had a very peculiar texture to it, its color contrasting with the paleness of *his* skin. And *his* wings… I always had been fascinated by not only their size, but also by the river of stars constantly flowing on them.

The man finally came out of his stupor and I saw him trying to get up, screaming insults and curses. But the winged creature forbid him this privilege so fast that even I didn't see the long foot crush the mad man's chest. The Angel bent slightly forward, holding *his* left hand out, pointing at him accusingly. *He* opened *his* mouth and a hard yet almost musical sound came out of it.

"Your name was added for revenge. Give it to me, and I shall save you. Deny me and I shall kill you, because it has been written."

But the man on the ground did not move, his hands around the Angel's ankle, grinning from the pain.

"Since you were a child, you have been dreaming of becoming a hero. Do you think you can do it with *it*? Very well then, you have made you choice."

The victim yelled a deafening scream as the Angel's toe nails changed into claws, long sharp blades plunging deep in the man's chest. The clothes and leather jacket quickly became soaked with the flowing blood just before the fabrics were suddenly torn from the aging body by an invisible force, revealing the Book apparently untouched by the crimson liquid.

Alas the tortured soul was not dead yet. He was agonizing, groaning and whining as his heartbeat was progressively slowing down.

The Dark Angel did not move when the train came right at them at a high speed. They both were hit, pulverized and the Book flew into shreds, lost forever.

Or so it seemed.

Later in the night, the news announced that the body of a man had been found on the railway next to an empty warehouse. He had apparently died of a heart attack and had collapsed on the rails.

No trace of the truth. The Book had disappeared but something was left on the rail, engraved in the steel next to the dead man's head.

Not a Hero, Unless you Die…

Decennium 00. Creation.

This summer rain was soft and welcomed on this little beach; the heat was unbearable in spite of the slight breeze. The sky had suddenly become darker, heavy clouds had taken their seats in front of the moon, arrogant satellite believing it could dominate the night by itself followed by its faithful stars.

With her large green eyes, she was looking far ahead of her, stepping lightly on the fine sand. Her long dark hair was flowing behind her in the wind as if it had a life of its own. She smiled as she looked up to the sky and she took her glasses off. She would not see as well, but it was better this way. Yes, much better. Slowly, she undid the buttons on her dress until it slid down her body. She walked out of it and kept going, now naked in the night.

She felt no shame; only a calm taking hold of her and growing with every passing second. What was this strange excitement running through her whole body? Was it from being naked on the beach, giving herself to the night and the wind, the rain water flowing on her skin? She stopped, moving her hands on her round arms before following the curves of her body down to her hips. *He* was here, *he* was calling her. *He* wanted her and she let herself be seduced. She let *him* touch her face, her neck, her breasts, her legs. No part of her body was left alone. She sighed and soon moaned as tears started to flow from her closed eyes. Was it pleasure or pain? Why this charming smile?

I was there when this young girl knelt on the sand then let herself fall on her back, her legs caressed by the constant flow of the sea, waves coming up and going back. The water was warm, going up to her waist before going away and coming back again. She was waiting. She was waiting for *him*. Her hands on each side of her head, she was giving herself to *him*, letting *him* choose of what *he* would do with her.

The water was now reaching her shoulders. Her face looking on one side, she was observing the horizon far away, waiting for *him* to move inside her, for *him* to make her *his* thing until *he* would fulfill the Book's will. Until *he* would respond to what she had written.

She had written her name following all the others an hour before already.

She moved her hand between her thighs, maybe that would make him appear faster. Soon her body started to move as water was covering her. Only her face was out of the water, giving her a bit more time. She was calling *him*. In a whisper at first, soon in a plaintive and sad moan.

He appeared finally, as though he was coming out of the water in the distance. A bright aura emanated from *him* such that even *his* robe and *his* hair seemed to glow. *He* leaned on her and moved *his* hands behind her back, lifting her to *his* soft and androgynous face. She sighed when *he* ran his hands on her body, soon going down between her legs.

They rose in the air as the Angel held her and they started spinning while *he* was gently kissing her long neck. Her head thrown back, she offered no resistance as she was giving herself to *him* totally, to the pleasure… and to Death. She moaned when *he* moved inside her slowly, bringing her higher in the sky, wrapping *his* wings around her as a rain of black feathers started to pour.

"Why did you write your own name in the Book? Was it because you wanted to die, or was it for me?"

The Dark Angel had spoken with *his* soft and unnatural voice in a strange yet harmonious tone. *His* victim did not answer, her sighs interrupted only by her faint sobs.

"You know a name cannot be erased once it has been written. Should I save you? Beg for your life and I shall, defy me and I will kill you."

She did not answer, her body shaken with spasms as her pleasure reached the higher spheres of her consciousness. The two figures slowly came back down on the sand. *He* gently laid her down and kissed her softly, caressing her with *his* long and thin hands.

I had picked up the young girl's glasses when she had dropped them on the sand. I liked them, I must admit. Thin golden frames engraved with interesting symbols. She was so much prettier with her glasses on. I waited for the Angel to stand up and moved to the still body. *He* moved away to let me pass and I was grateful *he* did. I leaned towards the naked figure and put the glasses back in front of the large eyes that seemed asleep. I reorganized her hair, moving some strands away from her beautiful face. I moved my hand down her cheek before getting up, looking up at the Angel who was much taller than I was. It was my turn to move away, to leave them alone so the Book's will might be executed. *He* looked down at the girl and smiled.

The Angel of Death did not move when the tide suddenly came up, covering the naked body.

Later in the night, the news announced that the body of a naked young girl had been found on the beach. She had just turned nineteen and had rented a cabin nearby to spend some vacation time with her friends who were supposed to join her the day after. Her body had no mark of any kind and the hypothesis of a rapist was to be excluded after the preliminary exams. She had probably passed out because of the extreme heat and had collapsed until the tide had claimed her life.

No trace of the truth. I knew the Book was not at her place anymore, it had probably vanished only to be found by someone else who would not understand it.

In the young girl's diary, on the last page, a line was written in a shaky hand.

There is no God!

Decennium 01. Evolution.

Such a long time. Such a long time since I had seen her. She must have been six or seven years old the last time it happened.

Her name was Aleyna and it was a very fitting name. She was the sweetest angel when she would look at me with her big blue eyes, so deep that I would lose myself in them. I still feel the contact from her soft, pale skin.

I was a teenager when she was born, but it was when she was around three years old that we started to love each other. My girl, my little girl, her soft voice and gentle laughter when she would tell me about the cartoon she had seen on TV the day before while I would never tire of brushing and styling her long and silky blond hair.

I loved the times when she would jump on my lap and cuddle while telling me about all those things a child can live. And she was living a lot. When she was not with me, she would be playing with other children, or by herself. She used to make up stories between her dolls and stuffed toys, and God knows she had so many that one could easily be lost in the jungle her room was.

She was the one I had to protect. To protect her from *him*. This had been the conclusion to these strange dreams filling my mind while I was asleep.

I was with her. We had found each other again after what had seemed an eternity, and we were walking, running, playing together hand in hand in this blurry world. Then we stopped for a moment to rest, sitting on the green grass of a strangely empty park.

When she wrapped her arms around my neck, some boys appeared around us, as though they had come out of nowhere, encircling us. Aleyna was taken away from me, although I could not say how that happened, and I saw her disappear in the distance, in the very unstable background. I was on my knees, looking around for my little girl with no success. I became more and more worried as my heart started to beat so hard that I could hear it in my ears.

Black feathers fell from the sky and a new young boy appeared only a few feet away from me, holding in his hand what seemed to be a gun. He was looking at me without any expression on his pale face. He suddenly aimed his weapon at me, and I didn't have time to think about what was happening as I was falling to the ground. My life was fading, darkness was coming around me, and I died.

But it was not over yet. In a bright flash of light, I was sent back to the very moment my little girl was taken away from me. Then this same boy, weapon in hand, threatening me with his empty eyes. When he aimed at me, a gun of the same kind appeared in my hand. I tried to dodge the bullet and shot at the boy. But I was not fast enough, and again I fell to the ground, dying.

One more time, the same scene. What was this all about? Was it some kind of trial, some kind of test? The same boy, the same weapons. But this time I reacted right away as though my subconscious had taken control of my body and I shot the boy while rolling on my side. Everything became white, so white it hurt my eyes. And a figure was coming towards me in this bright light. Aleyna was running back to me, her beautiful smile illuminating her face. I joined her and took her in my arms, holding her as close as I could, repeating her name as tears were flowing down my face.

I woke up in tears and covered in sweat, stunned by this dream which had been one of the most terrifying I ever had. Then I saw *him*.

The black-winged Angel I knew so well, the Angel I was supposed to follow everywhere *he* would go so I could be the witness of the Book's will. When a name was written after all the others, I knew where I would find this creature in charge of giving death. I had no power over *him* or over the Book but they could not do anything against me either, at least not directly. I was the witness, the observant. I was the one who knew the truths the world did not want to see. I was living in another world.

I sat up in my bed, grabbing a cigarette, and I knew.

Her name had been written after all the others an hour before already.

The Angel was looking at me coldly, glowing in *his* black clothes, *his* skin almost transparent. *He* was here to make sure that I would not fight *him*, that I would not step out of my role to save her while nothing or no one could go against the Book's will.

No name had ever been erased from the Book after being written or appearing. I knew it.

A child's bedroom. I was sitting on the cupboard made of plain wood, looking at the darkness. A small bed could be seen, a small chest full of toys next to it. She was there, asleep, her chest moving up and down under the blanket as she was breathing slowly. Her long blonde hair was spread all over her pillow. She had just turned ten years old a few days prior. I knew that but I had not been able to contact her, it was forbidden to have any relation with the living.

A curtain of glowing black feathers came out of nowhere, covering the floor as the great wings were being materialized seconds before the tall body. The Angel looked at the Book on the desk, open to the page where the little girl's name was written. *He* leaned above her and put *his* white hand on her forehead, pushing a few strands of hair out of the way. *He* ran *his* fingers on her cheeks all the way down to her chin. She moved a little during her sleep, as though she was dreaming. Her eyes rolled in their orbits as the dream was changing into a nightmare.

It was unbearable to see what was going through this little girl's mind, monsters hiding under her bed or in the closet before they would come out to eat her alive. Where did these dreams come from? Were they produced by the television showing more and more violent programs, where even cartoons are made of monsters that need to be destroyed at all cost? Or was it the Angel *himself* giving her these hideous images so *he* could terrify the mind before taking the body?

I couldn't take it anymore as *his* marble fingers were moving from her cheeks to her neck, soon reaching the small shoulders. *He* was measuring the level of the soul *he* had come to claim, figuring out what would happen of the Book after she died.

I got up, coming down from the cupboard and slowly walked towards the little girl's bed. *He* saw me, and as usual when I was entering the scene, *he* let me pass almost respectfully. I looked at *him* with eyes I wanted to be cold before bringing them to the little girl, now sleeping peacefully. She looked beautiful in her flannel pajamas, covered by thick blankets that were making her too warm.

His voice resonated in my mind as a barely perceptible whisper, a soft and melodious tune, yet cold and heavy.

"How dare you? Don't you know after all these mortal years that no one can go against the will of the Book? What are you trying to do, save her? You could not save your precious Annabella when her name was in the Book, you will not be able to stand in front of that little girl either."

There was no need to remind me. There was no need to remind me that my heart and my soul were still bleeding from witnessing the death of one I had loved so much when I was still part of this world, before the Book itself came to claim me and elected me as the one who had to watch those deaths only to report to this same Book.

But not her. God no, not *this* little girl. If I had any powers, I had to use them to save her from her bed of black feathers. I had to save her from those horrible dreams, no matter the Angel's fury toward me, no matter the Book's or even God's wrath.

I turned around to face the Book as I felt the little girl becoming agitated behind me. The Book seemed to glow, as though it had a life of its own and the pages started to turn themselves, slowly at first then faster as if a breeze was blowing on them. It finally stopped on a page where my name was glowing in golden letters, showing how different I was from the thousands of other names in the Book.

The Angel moved *his* dark eyes in my direction, the cold tune echoing in the room.

"It is the first and only thing that will be granted to you. Then your immortal life will be devoted to the Book, as it should already be. Her name will be erased, but under one condition. You will never be part of this girl's life ever again; you will not interfere with her life in any way ever again. Fail to honor this and you shall be destroyed along with her."

After *his* last words, *he* started to fade; his image lost its consistency until it completely disappeared along with the Book in a warm breeze hitting my face.

"Is that you?... Is that really you?..."

The little voice had emerged from behind me. This crystal voice, its slow pace and calm tone that used to put me to sleep many years before. I turned around slowly to face the figure who was now sitting in the bed as I felt the tears roll down my cheeks. I had no real body in this world. But she could see me, I could feel her hand on mine as if she was calling me.

"Aleyna my dear…" I whispered as I fell to my knees, grabbing the small face in my hands to kiss her forehead.

"That's really you, you came back!" She said with a widening smile on her face and brightening eyes.

I looked at her for the longest time, not able to say a single word. I brought her against me, hugged her as hard as I could. Then I brushed her silky blonde hair with my hand, ran my fingers on her face, kissed her forehead again. I had missed those contacts so much, I was now aware of it. And I would miss them even more now that I knew she could see me, that to her I was not just an ethereal entity, a breeze or a picture taken out of a too imaginative mind.

"No my dear… I'm not coming back… I am only a dream, a

dream to chase your nightmares away. I'm here to say goodbye, to tell you that I love you no matter where I am or where you are."

She looked at me with her big bright blue eyes before putting her small hand on my cheek to wipe the tear that was rolling down. She started crying as well, and it was more than I could bear.

"I won't see you again then…" She said between sobs.

I kissed her forehead and her cheek one last time before moving my hand in front of her eyes to put her back to sleep as I brought the blankets back over her.

"No you won't my dear… Because… *We don't live in the same world…*"

Decennium 02. Adaptation.

He was sleeping peacefully, lost in his erotic and dirty dreams where the main topic was the fear of his victims and the horrors going on, following the twisted path of his imagination. He had gone to bed late, barely conscious that he was home as the drugs and alcohol he had taken had blurred his mind and clouded his perception of things surrounding him. He barely remembered what he had done that night. Others would remember for him…

His day was not very different from the others making up most of his miserable existence. He got up late and wandered in the town with no real goal, going to the same stores to talk to the same worthless people that were populating his world. Then by the end of the afternoon he received a call from a friend who seemed to have turned better than he did. His friend invited him to spend the evening at his place to share a drink. The parents were supposed to be away for a few days on the other side of the country, and the younger sister would be gone for most of the night with one of her girlfriends. Rendezvous was set up and they met each other as planned.

His name was Frank. He was sitting on the armchair facing his friend Max, who had invited him and was sitting on the white leather sofa. The discussion would only die out when they would light up a cigarette or pour a new drink, the topic being as insignificant as they themselves were.

Frank had short brown hair, his dark eyes reflecting only his lack of real personality. His face, not shaven for several days, had strong features, almost elegant. He was a good looking man for sure; he knew it and used it to his advantage.

Max was his complete opposite with his light blonde hair and his blue eyes which seemed to shine with intelligence even though none was really to be found behind them. He was telling a joke as he took out a Ziploc bag from his pocket. In the plastic bag was some kind of dried plant shaped in brownish ball about as big as a bubble-gum. The kind of drug young people liked to smoke to feel "relaxed". After a few simple manipulations, he ground part of it and placed it on a sheet of cigarette paper that he rolled almost without looking at it. He brought it to his lips and lit it with a lighter that was lying on the table in front of him until now.

They smoked for a while, taking turns until they started to have totally random conversations as they kept drinking their alcohol.

Max started to talk about a book he had found on one of the brick walls at school. It seemed to be a very old book, its cover made of thick leather, the binding sewn. Each corner of the cover was reinforced with protective ornaments apparently made of gold or some close metal; the pages seemed to be made of a really good quality parchment. There was no title to it, nothing was written on the cover. Its content was the interesting part of it though. It was about half full of names written the same way old priests and monks would transcribe and copy manuscripts before a more modern printing process was invented. First names and last names, nothing else, never more than one full name for each line. There was no indication whatsoever as to what it could have been.

"*It makes no sense...*" He said simply. "What's the use of making such a list of names?"

"Maybe it's a kind of registry, like for births or something..." Frank replied.

"Or for deaths!" Max objected before laughing. "Who knows, maybe we'll have our names in there too someday!"

They both laughed at the joke without knowing that they were closer to the truth than they ever imagined.

It was at that time that Max's younger sister came in the apartment as she was coming back from the party she had attended at her friend's place. She looked tired but smiled to the young men, leaning forward to kiss her brother on the cheek.

At fourteen years old, she was quite pretty, already blooming into a nice young woman. Not exactly tall, but thin, her long silky blonde hair framing her pale face with two blue jewels of eyes. She got rid of her coat, showing herself in a white shirt and tight black pants. Her brother invited her to sit with them and she moved to the sofa, plopping down with a sigh, telling them how boring her evening had been. She was speaking with that crystal voice that was only hers. She pretended not to pay attention to the heavy smell of drugs floating in the room. She was almost used to it, as it seemed that indulging in this kind of recreational activities was her brother's favourite hobby when their parents were away.

I still remember my literature and philosophy classes at school, when were put into our brains all these authors and philosophers who had thought a series of truths after they studied the world surrounding them. I must admit I liked some of the ideas. Jean Jacques Rousseau had some very special theories of his own about human nature. He would write something along the lines of "Man is naturally good, society corrupts him." To deny or confirm this theory could seem easy, but is it really?

Max asked the young girl if she wanted something to drink, and although she hesitated, she accepted with one of her beautiful smiles.

Did Mr Rousseau, from the top of his heavens, see Max drop a white pill in the orange soda he was pouring? Did Mr Rousseau see the smirk on this blonde young man's face as he was watching the girl drink, feeling scrutinized by two pairs of blurred eyes, as she kept the glass close to her mouth in an attempt to escape the horrid smell of drugs? She even came to think that the smell was coming from her drink at some point.

After a few minutes, her vision became blurry and she could only hear vague echoes of a conversation between the two men who were still staring at her with an interest she didn't understand. Her thoughts could not seem to be able to stick to her mind. She wanted to say something, that she was not feeling well, but no sound came out of her slightly open mouth. She was only aware of her slow and difficult breathing as the image of the living room was dancing, undulating in front of her dizzy eyes. She didn't feel the glass slip off her hands, the liquid covering her shirt and her pants.

When her brother asked her if she was alright, she only heard distant sounds. She could not protest when the blonde man leaned over her and started to unbutton her shirt, saying that she needed to be changed. It felt like a light breeze on her body when he cupped the small breasts after removing her bra.

Frank looked miserable, running his hand in his dark hair, barely able to understand the situation he was in. He tried to say something against it, but was not really convincing when he saw his friend take her sister's pants off of her and drop them on the floor.

It is often said that reason has its reasons it itself ignores. What is reasonable, what is not? Each individual is different and for each, the border doesn't seem to be at the same level. Is Man really naturally reasonable?

Frank made a sound again when Max, the evil smirk still on his face, slid his hand between the slightly spread thin legs. The young girl didn't object as the only thing that could be heard from her was her weak breathing. Her mind was fighting to come back to the surface, to understand what was happening to her body. Her brother got up only to remove the last piece of clothing that was protecting her before laying her down on the sofa, meeting no resistance as he did so.

"She doesn't seem to dislike it." He said with a smile on his face as he ran his hand on the small breasts before bringing it down between the teenager's legs, touching her most intimate part.

Did she see me? Could she see me as she turned her face towards me, her beautiful eyes glowing with emptiness while her molesters were taking off their own clothes? She looked like she was imploring me with her empty gaze that was piercing through my very soul. But I knew she couldn't see me, her mind was gone from her body.

She shivered when the first one moved inside her, destroying her even though she was not conscious of it. A tear rolled down from her closed eyes and I started to cry as well, swearing to avenge her, to make them pay in the most horrible way I could possibly be capable of.

You will never be part of this girl's life ever again; you will not interfere with her life in any way ever again. Fail to honor this and you shall be destroyed along with her.

It was late in the night when the majestic Angel materialized at last in this miserable bedroom in spite of all the modern equipment. The computer was humming weakly in the corner, the light from the screen flashing with orange tones.

For the first time in this life, I had waited for *him* with impatience; I had wanted to see the large winged figure appear in this rain of black feathers that had become such a routine for me. I could act alone in this kind of situation only if the Angel allowed it, which *he* usually did. But would *he* allow it today considering my implication with the next victims? It was not about reorganizing hair or bringing back a lost item. It was about death.

When *he* was fully materialized, *he* gave me a soft look, forcing me to come out of the shadow where I was standing, taking a few steps towards him. *He* probably understood what feelings must have made my dark eyes glow. It probably was the reason why *he* himself stepped back in the shadows, as though giving me *his* approval.

The young girl was sleeping in her bed next door, where I had put her, covering her naked body with her blankets. My anger, my ha-

69

tred was making me shiver, my limbs felt numb, shaky. With the drug in her system, there was no chance she would be woken up while I would proceed with my deed. But what about tomorrow when she would wake up and find herself naked in her white bed sheets, when she would finally be able to feel her body, finding out what had happened to her.

Frank had gulped one last drink before leaving, barely looking at the naked young body on the sofa. They had not even had the decency of putting her back in a more modest position as though in spite of being unconscious she was offering herself again. But all in due time, I had thought when he had left the smoky room.

With vague eyes, the girl's destroyer came in his room. He walked right through my ethereal body before sitting on his bed. In a few moves he got rid of his clothes before staying still, looking in my direction. It was that time I chose to appear to him since the Angel and the Book had given me this opportunity. He was startled at first but regained his composure, quickly getting up with a newborn energy. I smiled at his futile and worthless thoughts. Why not after all, I could answer his silent questions.

"I've had no name for a long time now." I whispered, barely moving my lips. "But I know yours. How? Look at this *useless* book, at the last written page."

Slowly, he did as commanded, grabbing the book from the nightstand's drawer. He stared at the last page for long seconds before looking back at me with surprise on his face, almost a form of stupor. It was pathetic really.

"You see, this Book is indeed some kind of registry for the deceased. All those whose names are on these pages are dead. You may not believe me, but the Book chooses its victims. It is some kind of God."

"I remember you now! You are…"

"Indeed." I said, cutting him off. "And I came back tonight to give you what you deserve. Death."

He leaped toward me with his head down, but only went through my ghostly body as I was laughing. I wanted to seem as perverted as he had been when he had taken off his sister's shirt a little while before. He looked at me with a scared expression on his face and grabbed a pair of scissors next to the computer keyboard. He tried to stab me with them but it was easy for me to stop him. I grabbed his wrist. With a simple and light pressure, I broke the bones in his wrist and he dropped his weapon, screaming. With his other hand he tried to loosen my grip on him but I would not budge. I made the scissors float in the air and grabbed them in my free hand.

Without any warning, I plunged the blades in his crotch before taking them out in a gush of blood. He screamed in pain but it only gave me more motivation to stab him in that very place once more, and again, and again. When I let go of him, he collapsed to the floor, moaning and whining, probably on the verge of passing out. I grabbed his hair and lifted him from the ground until his face was at my level. I showed him my free hand as my nails were slowly changing into claws, becoming longer and longer, shiny and sharp blades. He really was pathetic.

Slowly, I cut the skin right under his eyes, which rolled in their orbits while his moans were becoming fainter. The blood flowing from his wounds looked like crimson tears, sincere tears; it was his body, his soul weeping. Then I sliced through his cheeks, following the lines left by his bone structure. I despised him, I hated him. A dog would not have eaten his flesh; he was too hideous for that.

I had enough of him and I stabbed my claws in his abdomen before pushing him away, slicing through flesh as I did so. He fell on his back, bathing in his blood while his guts now outside his body were still palpitating

I finally turned to the Angel who was staring at me, his face blank of any expression.

"Was this torture necessary?" He whispered in his melodic tune.

"He's going to die in a few minutes anyway, it doesn't matter anymore." I answered in a cold voice I barely recognized as mine. "Let us go see the other, his name was written a few seconds ago."

He was sleeping peacefully, lost in his erotic and dirty dreams where the main topic was the fear of his victims and the horrors going on, following the twisted path of his imagination.

What was this pain I felt at the top of my back? It didn't matter at that moment; I would kill him as well. He would be the last act of my revenge, of this young girl's revenge.

I brutally woke him up, grabbing him by the collar of his dirty t-shirt and threw him on the floor. In a split second he was on his feet, looking all around him. With the same violence, I wrapped my hand around his neck, lifting him from the ground and pushed him against the wall that shook under the shock. I threw my fist in his ribs and he screamed in pain. Then I threw him back on the floor. He tried to catch his breath but was doing a poor job at it. I wanted to finish this quickly, and so I grabbed him by his hair and pulled his head back, breaking the bones of his neck as I did so. I plunged my claws in his throat. Blood flowed but I didn't take the time to observe it, slicing through the neck of this pitiful being.

His head rolled on the ground and his body collapsed. His eyes now empty of all life were staring back at me, a look of despair in them, so pathetic. Yet so honest, *reasonable*.

The young girl stopped talking, refused to eat, move, or sleep. This was attributed to the death of her brother who had probably died of a drug overdose, judging by the syringe found next to his body. His friend had apparently committed suicide in his apartment.

No trace of the truth. The bodies had been found intact, lying about the bloody scene that had occurred for each of them.

My back was hurting more and more, but I couldn't help looking at this pretty blonde young girl through the window of her room. She was sitting in a corner, knees on her chest and arms around her legs. Inside, she was glad that her brother was dead because she couldn't have faced him herself. But she could not bear her body anymore. What had been done to her was in her mind and would never leave her. She wanted to die as well.

She opened her mouth slightly, her soft voice barely audible.

"You came to avenge me... Why dying?... *It makes no sense...*"

Decennium 03. Development.

Alone, once again. She was standing in the middle of her room, in this darkness peculiar to winter times. She was facing the window, observing the snow that was falling in silence, covering the buildings and roads with its thick white coat as passersby were hurrying, wishing to be in the warmth of their homes, in front of their television. Alone in her comfortable bedroom, she was studying. She was looking at life unfolding in front of her when she knew she was about to die.

Her name had been written after all the others an hour before already.

But why the golden letters? Of all the names on these pages, only one had been written with such ink. The name of the one she had loved, that she still loved even though he was gone. Did that mean she would see him again, at last? Would he come himself to take her, to push her beyond the boundary between life and death?

He had killed her brother; she had seen it in a dream. She had seen the crimson blood leaving the mutilated body. Her brother's blood. She hated him so much that she thought she would be capable of torturing him herself. This damn brother who had drugged her before raping her with no remorse. He only had what he deserved. And all those stupid people who knew nothing, who understood nothing.

He knew, he understood. He had seen and he had avenged her with a terrible hatred.

I was there when she opened the Book once more, the tip of her fingers running on her name as though seeing it again would bring her the last answer. I observed her from one of the dark corners of her room, seeing only her back; slim figure in the darkness, glowing blonde hair. I remembered those times we spent in this room, playing as we were sitting on the floor while she was making up worlds and stories, laughing with her crystal voice. It was a bit before the Book had chosen me to be the witness of Death itself.

The Angel would not come tonight. I knew it, although the reason for it was not clear. She had to die, and I was the one who had to take her. Maybe it was my last punishment. What was to happen, what would become of me when this teenager would disappear? She was the only living being left that I still loved in spite of my own immortality. Would I become as insensitive as the Angel *himself*, supposed to take lives without saying anything? Kill with a cold indifference, no matter the person or the reason. Was the Angel a creation of Man, of God, or of the Book itself? Was *he* alive before being the messenger of Death? I had no idea then, and I don't know any more today.

The young girl turned around slowly until she was facing me, pulling me out of my thoughts as my eyes met hers, the blue of her irises almost glowing in the dark. Her pale skin contrasted with the lack of light in the room, as did her blonde hair and her eyes. She could not possibly see me where I was standing, blending with the darkness. At most she may have been able to distinguish a vague figure; some very sensitive people could do that much about the Angel or myself. But she *knew*. She could feel me and the expression on her face was only confirming it.

"That's you, right?..." She said in a whisper. "You're here, right?"

I took a step forward so she could see me finally while I was trying to hide all those feelings being stirred inside me. She moved toward me. I had not expected such serenity coming from her at that very moment. I was ready for her tears, but none came. She put her hand on my chest as though making sure I was real before moving it to my cheek, her big eyes looking deep into mine. She was the only one capable of seeing me without me doing anything for it, she was the only one able to touch me as though I was human, made of real flesh. Maybe that was the reason why I had to take her, her life, her soul…

Slowly, she embraced me, hugging me tight against her, and she started to cry in silence. After what seemed an eternity, she let go of me and took a few steps back to look at me from head to toe while I was standing here, staying as still as a statue.

"Aleyna…" My voice resonated in a never ending echo in the small bedroom.

"You came to kill me, right?" She said as she turned around slightly to look by the window. "You're here because my name is in the Book, right after my brother and his friend…"

"I don't want to kill you…" I replied as I turned to her bed.

This bed where she was sleeping when I was granted the wish to save her from the Angel. This bed from where she had seen me for the first time as I was standing now. It had been four years already.

"But you have to. You saved me once. This time you won't be able to…"

A sad smile formed on her lips as she was saying those words, powerful words in the mouth of this teenage girl. I did not know what to reply then, and I could not answer her question about the golden letters her name was written with.

She turned toward me once again, the moon forming some sort of supernatural aura around her blonde hair. The pain in my back felt stronger than before, so much that I couldn't help but grin because of it. Aleyna didn't seem surprised by what she was seeing. It was as if she knew.

"I dreamt it…" She whispered softly, answering my silent question. "You came to get me and to bring me to your world so we could be together again. You would embrace me with your wings…"

She came closer again and she kissed me softly as though she had always been waiting for that moment. I was crying. I could not kill her… No matter the Book's or the Angel's wrath, it was beyond me.

It felt like as though I was stabbed in the back, or rather that my back was tearing up from the inside. Pain became so unbearable that I fell to my knees. Aleyna stepped away from me, her eyes never leaving me, her face surprisingly blank of any expression although her eyes and cheeks were still wet from her tears.

I saw the first black feather flying around in front of me until more of them suddenly filled the dark room. And I felt the weight in my back as everything became so clear.

Wings. Deep black wings had appeared in my back. And so I had become *him*.

Aleyna was still staring at me, seemingly unmoved as a feather landed on top of her head. She gave me the most beautiful smile I had ever seen before saying:

"Good evening, Angel…"

Decennium 04. Decline.

It was already late in the night when he walked into his office, slamming the door behind him and loosening his necktie with a sigh before taking his jacket off. He moved to the ornamented cupboard and opened one of the doors, revealing the place where he kept several bottles of various alcohols. His favourite was whisky. He even imported it directly from Scotland, not wanting to bother with standing in line at the liquor store. He grabbed the bottle and one of the glasses next to it before stepping toward his desk. He poured himself some of the golden liquid and sat down, holding the glass in the air for a few seconds, his eyes closed as though he needed some time to reflect on whatever was going through his mind. Finally, he sipped some of the drink and sighed again in satisfaction before bringing the glass down on the desk's wooden surface, still holding it in his hand.

It had been a good day for him. He had been able to strike a deal that would bring him millions of dollars for the next few years. He had secured a comfortable future for himself, and for his family. He had had to bend a few rules, but that shouldn't be a problem if nobody looked too closely at the fine prints. And he would be able to send his children to the best universities he himself had never been able to afford as a student. In the end, it was all worth it, and he had no regret.

He opened one of the drawers, searching for some papers. A frown formed on his face as he pulled a thick black book that seemed to be hiding under other folders and notebooks. He didn't remember ever owning such a book, and wondered what it was doing there, or who placed it there. His secretary would usually leave things to be checked on the top of the desk, not inside. He opened it and was puzzled by what he was looking at. A list of names, one full name per line, was filling up about half the pages. Nothing else.

He shrugged and closed the book, looking at the metal ornaments protecting each corner for a few seconds before placing it back into the drawer. He would ask his secretary in the morning.

What he had not noticed though, was that his name had been written after all the others. And it had been an hour already.

I appeared on the other side of his desk, in the middle of the room. The black feathers from my wings preceded me, as though raining down from the ceiling and covering the expensive carpet. I remained silent as the man was staring at me, probably not believing his eyes, or wondering if he was dreaming. When I looked around, ignoring my prey for the moment, I finally saw her. She was sitting on the sofa by the door, her legs crossed and her arms spread on the back of it as though she actually owned the place. Her deep blue eyes were fixated on me and a smile formed on her lips. She waved lightly at me before bringing her hands on her knees. She tapped her wrist with one of her fingers as though she was silently telling me that time was pressing, or that I was late. I turned back to face the man who still had no idea what was going on. He could not see her sitting there, only I was able to.

It has been years since I took her life with my own hands. It had been both a punishment and a reward granted by the Book. At least it felt like it at the time, and I never linger on the reasons. Maybe I am afraid to discover what the real motives for the Book's existence are, or maybe I know them all too well but refuse to acknowledge them.

It has been a punishment because I had to kill Aleyna, and it tore me apart. But it has been a reward because since then, I am able to see her almost every day. The Book had probably deemed me capable of carrying the Angel's burden, and had elected my little girl as my watcher. But it also means that she has to watch me take countless lives, sometimes brutally when my victims struggle.

She hasn't aged, and neither have I. Even after all those years, she still looks like the fourteen years old girl she was when I took her life. An ever aging soul trapped in a teenager's body. Although it doesn't really affect us as we have no real use for our bodies. Or rather, we cannot really use them to interact with the living in ways you can.

The man sprung up from his chair and walked around the desk, shouting words I did not understand, or rather that I did not listen to. When he was close enough, I wrapped my hand around his neck and lifted him off the ground. He struggled and tried to fight back, but it all didn't matter to me. His life flashed in front of my eyes, from his very first memory as a child to the time when I appeared to him just a few minutes prior.

I never understood this ability that was given to me along with my dark wings. It happens every time. It only lasts for a second or two, but it usually is enough for me to know absolutely everything about my victim. The good and the bad. It feels as though I am supposed to judge that person, to decide whether they are worth killing or not. Yet my judgement does not matter, the Book already made the decision and there was nothing to be done about it. Except death. At most, it helps me decide if I want to be gentle with them, or not.

And Aleyna has to watch it all, every single time, just as I was the Angel's witness before her. It scares me sometimes to see that she almost seems to enjoy it. There are moments when I catch a glimpse of her as she is intently staring at me, a faint smile on her thin lips. What will become of her, of us?

Are we condemned to this life for eternity, taking souls indiscriminately, no matter if the person is good or evil, no matter their age or race, from infants to old men? Then what? Will there be a time when the Book decides that I am no longer useful and that the flame should be passed on to a new generation? To Aleyna?

I almost hope so. And if that's the case, my desire is that she puts me out of my misery herself. I know she would object and possibly defy the Book. But that is what I wish for even though I am not allowed to wish for anything anymore.

And many years after she takes my place, she will be replaced as well and her soul will finally join mine. It is the cycle imposed by the Book, because no matter what,

The Angel deserves to die...

Decennium 05: Extinction

The Guardians
Of Wonderland
Preview

THE GUARDIANS OF WONDERLAND

preview

A note from FSan regarding the following story:

What you are about to read is a preview of the first few pages taken from my upcoming novel project titled "The Guardians Of Wonderland".

Please consider that this is still a work in progress, and that the following text may not be transcribed as such in the final publication. As I am about to publish "When The Angel Deserves To Die", I am still actively writing "The Guardians" and it is not quite near completion yet. Many things still have time to change, including what you are about to read

I do hope that you will enjoy this excerpt, and I cannot wait to complete the final book and to share it with my readers.

July 2014

1.

He didn't think he would ever feel this way, but today he almost missed his city. The streets crowded with some of the worst drivers in Canada –or so he thought at least. The Skytrain about to burst on game nights, the dirty sand of English Bay. Even the useless overpriced shops on Robson Street that covered themselves with heavy iron curtains at night since the last riot a few years back. He enjoyed hanging out with his small group of friends on the square area near the Art Gallery, on the corner of West Georgia and Hornby. Particularly in the evening, when the night would take over the sun hidden by thick clouds, when the street lights would come to life in a familiar buzzing sound. While Downtown seemed to go to sleep as most of the population lived in the neighbouring cities or in the residential quarters of Vancouver.

It usually wouldn't stay quiet for long though as a different kind of people would come to life, wandering the streets aimlessly, or so it seemed. You would see the occasional homeless man searching for a place to sleep like an air vent that would keep him warm for a few hours until some arrogant policemen would walk by and kick him awake, ordering him to find another spot. But the most part of the crowd at night was composed of the clubbers, men and women of all ages going to lock themselves up in cramped and noisy places, gorging their livers with alcohol while rubbing themselves against each other. Maybe snort a line of coke in the filthy bathrooms before going back to their senseless and disarticulated dances. It was called "socializing". He called it "the circus".

He had named the girls "the clowns" with their faces plastered in makeup and their bodies wrapped in mismatched and colourful apparels, speaking in nasally voices as though they talked while pinching their nose. The guys, on the other hand, were "the buffoons", trying to get the girls' attention any way they could think of, hoping they would get laid or at least leave with a fake phone number. All this was ridiculous and entertaining at the same time.

In his nineteen years, he had never really left Vancouver beside the occasional trip to popular destinations nearby such as Whistler or Vancouver Island. The only times he had left the country were to go to Seattle, south of the border. His parents made regular visits there to see friends living in the area, but also to go shopping as prices were generally cheaper and Washington State taxes not as high as the ones in British Columbia.

Today's trip was different though, and much longer –at least it felt like it to him.

"Jack!" his father called without taking his eyes off the road.

The young man blinked once and shook his head slightly as though he had been awaken abruptly. He didn't answer, instead just looking at his father, his vision taking its time to come in focus.

"Give me a smoke." The older man said, bringing two fingers to his lips as though already smoking an invisible cigarette. "I finished my pack and I forgot to buy a new one before leaving."

Jack shrugged before searching through his pockets until one of his hands came back up holding the red cardboard box covered in pictures and slogans supposed to convince the already addicted that smoking is bad for you. His favourite was the image of a green gloved hand holding a human heart –or was it a lung- with the phrase "Smoking causes a slow and painful death" in big and bold letters. It always made him laugh when he saw that one.

"You buy me a pack too later, then." He said while getting one of the cigarettes out.

"I'm just asking for one, not fifteen. Asshole."

"High demand, low supply. What is rare, is expensive." Jack said with a smirk on his face, waving the white tube in front of his father's nose.

"I'll remember that next time you ask me for gas money so you can sneak in your girlfriend's house to get laid. Or try to, rather."

"Fucker."

The man looked at his son with a smirk of his own and grabbed the cigarette. He brought it to his mouth, pinching the filter between his lips.

"That's right, boy. I'm pretty sure I get it more often than you do." He said, punctuating his sentence with the click of his lighter.

"At least I don't need blue pills." Jack replied looking away at the road, lighting a cigarette as well before rolling his window down.

Jack's father worked in the real estate business, so he had decided to go check out that house himself. He had been thinking about buying a new house for a few years but the market had not been favourable, until now. Things in the world were finally calming down, people were becoming more confident and less reluctant to open their wallets. The general economy was on the rise again and everything seemed more affordable even though they were not really.

The last war in Europe had ended a couple of years earlier. It had been a short one, but a brutal one. Most of the Eurozone had collapsed and so had the currency which ultimately affected the whole world. What had started as insurrections in France soon contaminated Spain and Greece before spreading throughout the continent. Several governments were overthrown and what appeared as a revolution of sort quickly became a full sized civil war. Other countries around the world felt that they had something to say about it. The United States and Canada had failed miserably in Eastern Europe and had no choice but withdraw their troops, redirecting their good intentions to Western Europe and changing the civil war into another World War, though some still refused to call it so.

Only this time there was no evil enemy to fight, nobody to free from tyranny and oppression, not even oil to gather. Only people discontent with their governments and their situations, only on a much higher level than it had been for decades before that.

Whenever the topic on the war surfaced, Jack never saved his words against the US and Canadian governments, claiming that they involved themselves for no real reason, without anybody asking for their help. He believed that they had sent more soldiers to their deaths only to make people forget about their failures in other parts of the world where they also had no business getting involved. But his father usually brushed the arguments aside, saying that Jack was too young and could not understand what the world was all about. "Because you know better? All you've done your entire life is go to College for a couple years and sell houses for the rest of your life." Jack would retort, which would make his father laugh.

It all did not matter anymore, except for the fact that the markets had been so low that they could only go up now. And Jack's father wanted to use that opportunity.

He wanted to buy another house though he had not decided where yet. His plan was to use it during his vacation time if the location was interesting enough, and rent it out the rest of the year before selling it in the future when prices would go higher again.

One of his contacts in Oregon had sent him details about a house that would possibly fit his criteria, and so he had decided to go look at it, dragging Jack along for the occasion.

A few hours later, and after a couple stops for gas and food, they arrived at their destination, to Jack's relief. His father wanted to see the house before dawn, especially considering that the lot was fairly isolated, situated a mile or two away from the suburbs of Portland. Jack argued that they were staying overnight anyway and that he was tired from the boring trip, but his father took none of it and convinced his friend to take them to the lot right away.

It was another thirty minutes until both cars pulled up in the driveway of a fairly decent sized building. Not necessarily huge, but a good size for a small family as Jack's father pointed out though the young man showed no sign of interest.

The two-story house was obviously pre-war, judging by the style and type of materials used. As he stepped out of the car, Jack let his gaze wander around, looking for something that would make him feel as though he was not in the middle of nowhere, miles away from civilization, about to enter an old house with two men he knew nothing about as the sun was getting closer to the top of the tree line. But it was pointless. If he was going to be murdered tonight, nobody would ever know about it. He moved closer to his father.

"Why is it the only house around here?" he asked. "There's a road leading to it, clearly it's not a farmhouse cause there's no fields around or no facilities whatsoever..."

His father's friend —another realtor, smiled and explained in a few words as though trying to make it simple for Jack. The house was part of a development project started a few years before the war. It had ultimately been put on an indefinite hold because of the conflict in Europe and investors getting scared. The house was supposed to be the demonstration house, something to show potential buyers and investors before they committed themselves (and their money) which would allow the project to actually be built. It was a common practice in the business. When everything collapsed and the project was pretty much abandoned, a young couple bought the place for cheap and lived in it with their teenage girl for a few years before vanishing.

"Hold on." Jack interrupted. "What do you mean, they vanished?"

"One day, they were just gone." the realtor said plainly. "Mortgage payments stopped coming in and when the bank sent their people to the door, nobody was here. By the time the bank got the house back, it had been empty for weeks, maybe even months." He shrugged with a smile. "They've been trying to sell it ever since but nobody from around here wants to hear about it. It's a good house, wait to see inside."

And without further explanation, the front door was unlocked and swung open as one of the realtors gestured to Jack and his father, inviting them to proceed.

It was a good house indeed, even Jack could tell as much. It almost smelled new still as though it had been built the month before and nobody had ever lived in it. "And now the fun begins." His father said to him in a whisper as he leaned towards him. Jack knew what it meant. His father and the other realtors were about to start talking legal issues, inspections reports, land value and other boring details. He rolled his eyes and pointed to a room, silently telling them that he was going to wander around and find something to do until they were done.

Ultimately, he ended up in the basement where extra furniture had been stocked underneath linens now covered in dust. He knew his father would end up selling most of those things and keep only the items he liked, as he always did. With a bored expression on his face, Jack lifted some of the linens to peek at some of the furniture. Mostly preassembled pieces probably coming from a cheap furniture store nearby. There was nothing of value as real wood was rarely used to make this kind of things anymore. But something caught his eyes at the back of the room. From afar, it looked like a full sized cupboard, but as Jack came closer he guessed what it actually was.

He pulled on the drape covering the piece, revealing a large mirror standing at least three feet taller than he was. Extending his arms, he could barely hold both sides of it at once. But what fascinated him was the heavy looking frame made of wood and metal. It almost looked alien as though such designs couldn't have possibly come from a human mind.

It had been carved, twisted shapes and lines, some of them made to look like monsters or body parts, or even representing sexual themes. At the top and middle of the frame, a heart-shaped face was surrounded by what looked like an octopus' tentacles, the whole thing made to look like a large eye staring at the watcher, the heart in the center being the pupil.

After a while, Jack started to feel almost uneasy looking at this, tracing some of the lines with his fingers. Until he finally let his eyes trail to the reflection of himself.

Behind him, through the mirror, he could see the rest of the basement barely lit by the single lamp attached to the ceiling. But the light seemed to flicker, occasionally throwing the room into darkness. When he turned around, the young man could only notice that the light bulb was perfectly fine and was shining the way it was supposed to. But when he looked back at the large mirror, the flicker continued, the darkness lasting longer with each time the light went off. Soon, Jack noticed that some of the covered furniture seemed to disappear from the reflection and the drapes were becoming dirtier. Was that blood drenching one of them in the corner? Now the whole reflection started to make waves, as though the glass was made of water and someone had disturbed its surface.

Jack moved closer, slowing moving his hand as if he was hesitant to touch the mirror. He heard someone laugh, a little girl's laughter. But it wasn't a laughter of joy… It was the laugh of someone who had gone mad.

"But we're all mad here!" Jack heard the little girl say even though he couldn't see her.

Jack shook as though he had been startled, and blinked. When he turned around, he stared at his father standing at the bottom of the stairs, calling him.

"What are you laughing to yourself about?" The older man said. "Come on, we're leaving." He added before walking back up the stairs without waiting for an answer.

Jack nodded and turned around again to look at the mirror one last time.

It was just an ordinary mirror with a strange looking frame.

A few drawings and sketches, because why not?

Muse

Thank you for reading.
Join me on
facebook (www.facebook.com/fsanporte)
and Twitter (@FSanPORTE)

www.ingramcontent.com/pod-product-compliance
Lightning Source LLC
Chambersburg PA
CBHW031845170626
46807CB00004B/1627